Copyright © 2023 by Storyshares. All rights reserved.

Black Rabbit Tales is an imprint of
Black Rabbit Books
P.O. Box 227
Mankato, MN 56001
www.blackrabbitbooks.com

This library-bound edition is published in 2025 by Black Rabbit Books, by arrangement with:

Storyshares, LLC
24 N. Bryn Mawr Avenue #340
Bryn Mawr, PA 19010-3304
www.storyshares.org

Printed in China.

The characters and events in this book are fictitious. Any similarity to real persons, living or dead, is entirely coincidental.

Library of Congress Cataloging-in-Publication Data
Names: Ford, Jennie (Children's author), author. | Quinton, James, author.
Title: Seashells, spice, and everything nice / Jennie Ford, James Quinton.
Description: Mankato, MN: Black Rabbit Books, 2025. | Series: These first letters | Focuses on letter blends: sc, sn, sw, sl. | Audience: Ages 10–14 | Audience: Grades 4–6 | Summary: "Sara and Destiny seem different at first, but their love of cooking helps them find what else they have in common. Together, they decide to make the world around them a better place"—Provided by publisher.
Identifiers: LCCN 2024023213 | ISBN 9781644668931 (library binding)
Subjects: LCSH: Readers (Elementary) | English language--Consonants--Juvenile literature. | Friendship—Juvenile literature. | Reading—Phonetic method—Juvenile literature. | LCGFT: Readers (Publications)
Classification: LCC PE1121 .F587 2025 | DDC 428.6/2—dc23/eng/20240624
LC record available at https://lccn.loc.gov/2024023213

**Aligned with the Science of Reading.
Interest Level: 4th grade and beyond.**

SEASHELLS, SPICE, & EVERYTHING NICE

JENNIE FORD
JAMES QUINTON

A DECODABLES CHAPTER BOOK

TABLE OF CONTENTS

JENNIE FORD	A PASSPORT FOR SARA	1
JAMES QUINTON	FROM DESTINY'S DESK	15
JAMES QUINTON	A FIRST FOR SARA	28
JAMES QUINTON	ADVICE FROM UNCLE STAN	41
JAMES QUINTON	FRIED CHICKEN FOR THE WIN	55

A PASSPORT FOR SARA

JENNIE FORD

Phonics Guide

"A Passport for Sara"

letter blends: sc, sn, sw, sl

sc
- school
- scanning
- scarlet
- scamper

sn
- snacks
- snorkel
- sniffed

sw
- sweets
- swim
- swing
- swan
- swished

sl
- slid
- sleek
- slip
- slumped
- sliver

high frequency words

- was
- were
- that
- with
- you
- would
- more
- thought
- some
- friends
- where
- different
- here
- them
- favorite
- family

challenge words

- vegetables
- school
- person
- history
- person
- learning
- Johnniecakes
- uncle

1

1

Sara lived with her Aunt Mal. Aunt Mal called her Sweets.

They lived on a sliver of a farm. The farm grew flowers and fruit and vegetables.

Sara loved it. Aunt Mal did, too.

Sara didn't go to school. The farm was her class. Some days Sara would slip a leash on her dog Cam.

She would fill up a basket with snacks and books.

They would scamper down a path to her secret place. It was a small pond under a blue sky.

There Sara slumped down on a swing and thought.

She read and studied. She spied swans swishing across the water.

She sketched. She sniffed at flowers.

On very hot days, she and Cam would swim.

One day Aunt Mal came home with a box. There was a scarlet bow on top.

"Surprise!" Aunt Mal yelled.

Sara stopped. She looked up from the pages she was scanning. "What is it?" she asked.

"Open it, Sweets," Aunt Mal said.

Sara did. Inside was a sleek, silver computer.

Aunt Mal smiled. "It's to help with your studies," she said. "But it's also a passport. You can use it to meet friends from other places!"

Aunt Mal set the computer on a table. She started it up. Sara slid in her socks around her.

"Here," Aunt Mal said at last. She stared up at Sara. "This is what I want you to see."

It was a website. There was a picture of happy teens. And a picture of letters.

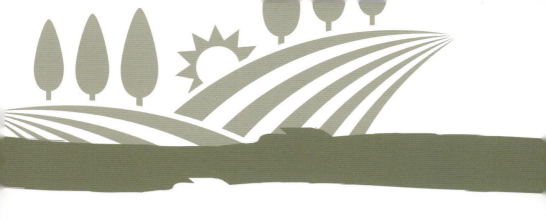

"It's called LEX," said Aunt Mal. "That stands for Letter Exchange. It's a way for you to meet other students your age."

Sara sat down and started to fill in a form. It asked all sorts of things. *Where was she from? What did she like to do?*

Soon, Sara met Destiny. Destiny was from the Bahamas.

At first, Sara thought she and Destiny were very different.

Sara was shy. Destiny was not. Sara lived on a farm in a small town. Destiny lived on an island. Destiny loved to snorkel and run. Sara loved to read.

But soon, Sara slowly started to see that she was a lot like Destiny.

Both girls loved to read. Both loved to swim and sketch.

And both spent a lot of time gardening and cooking.

They sent recipes with their letters. Like the girls, some were very different.

Sara had never tried Stew Chicken. That was Destiny's favorite food.

Destiny had never had pimento cheese. Sara used that in many dips.

But also like the girls, some of the recipes were the same.

Sara and Destiny both cooked grits. And they both cooked cornbread.

Destiny called it "Johnniecakes."

"What do I smell?" Aunt Mal asked one night.

Sara smiled. In her hand was a card for Destiny. It had a recipe Sara was making for Destiny to try. "Banana custard," Sara said.

Aunt Mal smiled. "Sounds good, Sweets."

From Sara's Kitchen

Servings: 8
Prep time: 10
Cook time: 15

Banana Custard

4 big eggs   1 tbs vanilla
2/3 cup milk   1 banana
1/3 cup sugar   1 oz butter
3 tbs cornstarch

Instructions:

Boil the milk in a pan. Add sugar. In a different bowl, mix the eggs and sugar. Add that to your pan. Stir for 3-5 minutes. Turn off heat. Add in banana and butter. Stir really, really good. Then put in the fridge for 30 min. Now eat!

Notes:

Hi Destiny! My uncle showed me how to cook this when I was ten. Now I cook it all the time. I hope you and your family like it.

JAMES QUINTON

FROM
Destiny's
DESK

FROM DESTINY'S DESK

JAMES QUINTON

| Phonics Guide

"From Destiny's Desk"

letter blends: st, sp, sk, sm

st
- Destiny
- stopped
- Stan
- stopping
- stack
- started
- esteem
- States
- stuff
- steps
- still
- last
- plastic
- forest
- list

sp
- inspected
- spotted
- spent
- spot

sk
- desk
- asked

sm
- smiled
- small

high frequency words

- she
- would
- want
- where
- coming
- asked
- looked
- about
- world
- have
- also
- said
- water

challenge words

- busy
- scrubbed
- favorite
- recipes
- pictures
- beach
- computer
- uncle
- camera

15

Destiny stopped. She inspected the clock. It was 6 p.m.

Uncle Stan said he would be home an hour ago.

What was stopping him?

Destiny got busy. She did not want to fret.

She spotted dirty dishes in the sink.

She scrubbed them and set them in a stack.

She spent some time at her desk.

It was her favorite spot. It's where she started TeenTalk.

TeenTalk was her video show. It was all about self-esteem. Over 10,000 fans loved her show.

Her desk was also where she sat to read and write letters.

She sent them to pals all over the world.

Destiny started to write to Sara. Sara was from the States.

Sara sent Destiny lots of stuff. Letters. Cards. Recipes.

Destiny smiled, then stopped.

There were steps coming her way. "Uncle?" she asked.

She went into the hall. Uncle Stan was home, at last. He was back from his trip with no fish.

Was that why he looked sad?

"What's the matter?" Destiny asked.

Uncle Stan sat and gave Destiny his phone.

On it were pictures of their favorite beach.

The sand was full of plastic bags and glass. There was trash in the water.

"How did this happen?" Destiny asked.

"People," Uncle Stan said. He looked small and sad. "They do not think about the land. Or the water. Or the animals. They do not see that this is the only world we have."

Destiny sat by her uncle. She was thinking. And thinking.

"Can I take this?" she asked at last. She was still holding Uncle Stan's phone.

He nodded.

"I will fix this," she said.

She went back to her desk in her room.

She opened her computer and saw her list of fans.

She turned on her camera. She was going to make a new show.

Destiny talked about the beach. She talked about growing up on it.

She talked about the animals she saw in the waters.

Then she showed the pictures on her uncle's phone.

At last, she clicked "end."

The show was now live.

"I hope this works," she said.

TeenTalk

by Destiny

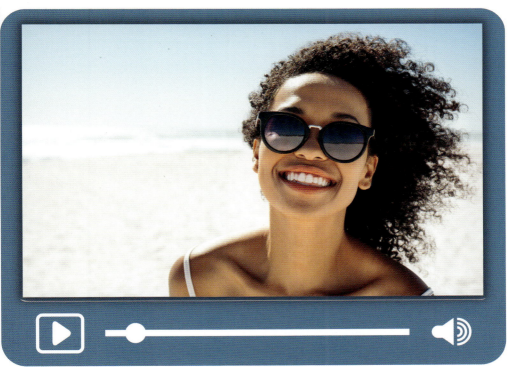

Destiny - The Beach I Call Home

9.2k views   1 day ago   #Beach   #WeCanFixThis

Tomorrow I will go to my beach to pick up the trash. I want to ask you to do that too. Go to your beach. Or go to your forest. Or go for a walk by your home. Just make the world a bit better. It's the only one we have got.

@MaxfromSeattle   45 min ago
I will def do this!

@SaraFromNC   8 hours ago
me too!

Add a comment....

A FIRST FOR SARA

JAMES QUINTON

| Phonics Guide

"A First for Sara"

letter blends: br, cr, gr

cr
- crisp
- crept
- crossed
- creek
- crew

br
- bring
- bridge
- broken
- branches
- brick
- breeze
- eyebrows
- brown

gr
- grin
- green
- growled
- grabbed
- grasp
- greatest
- grinned

high frequency words

- into
- off
- over
- because
- asked
- world
- soon
- about
- was
- water
- would
- writes

challenge words

- main
- pizza
- beach
- join
- nervous

28

The wind was crisp.

"Bring a jacket," Aunt Mal said. Sara did.

They got into Aunt Mal's car.

Sara opened her map with a grin. "Turn left," she said.

And then they were off.

They crept past green hills.

They crossed a bridge over a creek.

They bumped over broken branches.

Soon, they hit the main roads.

Soon after that, Sara's belly growled.

Aunt Mal saw a place called "Lunch Crew."

They stopped. Aunt Mal grabbed a green salad.

Sara asked for a brick oven pizza. Then they got back on their way.

They were going to the beach because of Sara's friend Destiny.

Destiny lived in the Bahamas.

She had a video show called TeenTalk.

On it, she had posted about her own beach. It was full of plastic and trash.

Destiny was going to do her best to fix it.

And she had asked her fans to do the same.

"Go into the world and make it better," Destiny said.

So Sara was.

It was the first time she would ever see the beach.

When they got there, Sara could hardly grasp what she saw.

The water went on and on and on.

The sand went on and on and on.

It was the greatest thing she had ever seen.

But then she looked closer.

There were broken bits of glass all over.

Trash cans were so full that some spilled.

It was just like Destiny's beach.

Sara got to work with Aunt Mal.

They grabbed some bags.

They started to pick up the trash.

Soon they had 3 big bags of it.

But there was a lot more to do.

"Maybe there is a way to get more help," Aunt Mal said.

"How?" Sara asked. She sat on the sand. The breeze felt good.

"Maybe you can get a crew to join us. Like Destiny."

Sara's eyebrows went up.

It was a good idea. But it made her scared.

Sara was shy. Destiny was not yet.

"You can write to her," Aunt Mal said. She knew Sara well. Aunt Mal could see that Sara was nervous. "Ask her for tips."

Sara would think about it. She grabbed her coat.

She went with Aunt Mal back to the car.

"I'll write to her tonight," Sara said.

Aunt Mal grinned.

From Sara's Kitchen

Servings: 25
Prep time: 5
Cook time: 2

Vinegar BBQ Sauce

2 cups vinegar   2 tbs ketchup
2 tbs brown sugar   1 tbs black pepper
1 tsp dry red pepper   1/2 tsp salt

Instructions:

Add all of it to a small pan. Bring to a boil. Let cool. Keep in a jar in the fridge.

Notes:

Hi Destiny,

I hope you like this recipe! I also want to ask you a question. I want to form a crew to help pick up my beach, like you have. But talking to new pals is hard for me. Do you have any tips?

Your friend, Sara

Advice
FROM UNCLE STAN

JAMES QUINTON

ADVICE FROM UNCLE STAN

JAMES QUINTON

| Phonics Guide

"Advice from Uncle Stan"

letter blends: pl, bl, gl, cl, fl

pl
- plopped
- plan

bl
- blue
- blew

gl
- glass
- glad

cl
- cloudy
- close

fl
- flip
- flops
- flipped

high frequency words

- wrote
- how
- friends
- there
- could
- would
- which
- meant
- pulled
- asked
- should
- anything

challenge words

- uncle
- docks
- smooth
- cloudy
- bucket
- pole
- special
- ocean
- matter
- esteem
- figuring
- happiness
- genius
- video

4

Destiny looked at Sara's letter. "I'm too shy," Sara wrote. "Do you have tips for how to make pals?"

Destiny tried to think.

How did she make friends? She did not know.

They were just sort of... there.

But Destiny knew who could help.

Uncle Stan always knew what to do.

He would be at the docks. It was morning time which meant he was trying to get fish.

Destiny plopped down on her bed.

Then she pulled on her flip flops. She blew the hair out of her face. And she left.

It was a warm, cloudy morning. The ocean was smooth like glass.

She found her uncle just where she knew she would.

He was sitting on a blue bucket. It was flipped over. His fishing pole was in his hands.

"Destiny!" he called. He smiled when he saw her. He looked glad to see her.

He pulled another bucket close to his side.

Destiny sat.

"What are you doing here?" Uncle Stan asked.

"I just got a letter from Sara," Destiny said. "She needs help. I knew you would have a plan."

Her uncle pulled in his line. He put his fishing pole down.

Then he looked at the letter from Sara.

"Ah," he said. "She wants to know how to make new pals. What do you think she should do?"

Destiny shrugged. "I do not know. I do not do anything special to make friends. I just... talk."

"About what?" her uncle asked.

"I do not know."

"Think."

"I... talk about the things that matter most to me. The ocean. Self-esteem. Taking videos."

"There you go," Uncle Stan said.

"I do not understand," Destiny said.

"I do not think Sara needs help making friends. I think she needs help figuring out what she loves. When you know what you love, you cannot help but talk about it. Your happiness attracts people. You do not even have to try."

Destiny thought that was genius.

She was glad to have a plan.

"I will write to her now!" Destiny said. She got up.

"Wait," her uncle said. "I bet there are a lot of people like Sara." He winked.

Destiny smiled. She knew what he was telling her to do. She ran home.

She opened her computer and started to record a new video.

This way was even better than writing a letter.

This way, she could share her uncle's advice with Sara. But she could also share it with all of her show's fans.

Destiny pressed a green button.

"I'm back," she said. "And I have something important to talk to you about today."

 **TeenTalk**

by Destiny

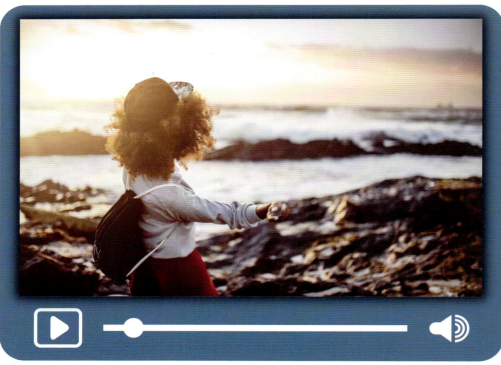

Destiny - Share the Love

 5.4k views 1 day ago #Friends #SelfEsteem

We can all make friends the same way. And it isn't hard. Even if you are shy. Here's the secret: Just talk about what you love. Being happy is like a magnet.

 @MaxfromSeattle   45 min ago
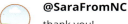

@SaraFromNC   8 hours ago
thank you!

Add a comment....

FRIED CHICKEN FOR THE *Win*

JAMES QUINTON

FRIED CHICKEN FOR THE WIN

JAMES QUINTON

Phonics Guide

"Fried Chicken for the Win"

letter blends: tr, dr, fr, pr

tr
- tried
- trip
- trays
- trunk
- try
- truly

dr
- drinks
- drive
- dry

fr
- fried
- front
- friends

pr
- prizes
- profits
- Priya
- protect
- surprised
- pretty

high frequency words

- long
- asked
- also
- about
- ocean
- love
- together
- think
- was
- they
- would
- there
- people
- great
- number

challenge words

- worry
- finally
- mouth
- advice
- organized
- nearby
- event
- stations
- arrive
- agreed
- announce
- definitely
- recipe

55

5

Sara tried not to worry. The day was finally here.

She and Aunt Mal packed drinks into the car.

They had a long drive in front of them. They were going back to the ocean.

"Ready for the trip? For new friends?"

Aunt Mal asked.

Sara's mouth felt dry.

She was happy, but also scared.

"I hope so," she said.

Sara had asked her friend Destiny how to talk to new people.

Destiny's advice? "Think about what you love and just tell others about it. Let your love do the work."

Sara and Aunt Mal had made a list of the things that Sara loved.

At the top of that list was cooking.

Together they had organized a cook-off.

It would cost $20 to enter.

There would be prizes and games.

And the profits would be put to cleaning up nearby beaches.

The sun had just come up when they got there.

Aunt Mal's friends were there.

They were putting grills and tables on the sand.

Sara started to get pots and pans and trays from the trunk.

There was another girl there. She looked to be about Sara's age.

She was hanging banners up.

"Go say hi," Aunt Mal said.

Sara gulped.

She walked over to the girl.

"Hi, I'm Sara," she said.

"I'm Priya," the girl told her.

"Those look great," Sara told her.

"Thanks. I'm really happy to be a part of this event!"

Sara smiled.

This was already going great.

Soon, the beach was covered in tables and cooking stations.

People were just starting to arrive.

"Priya, would you pass out tickets to our new friends?" Sara asked.

Priya nodded and went to the gate.

"It looks like it's going to be a big day," Aunt Mal said.

Sara agreed.

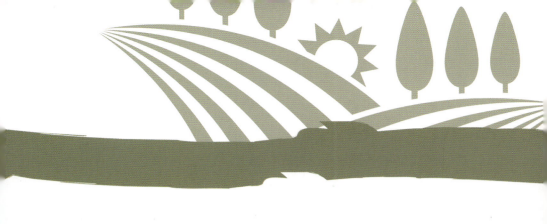

The rest of the day was filled with music and good food.

Sara and Priya worked hard.

But they also found time to try all the different dishes. And talk. Sara did what Destiny said. She talked about all the things she loved.

By the end of the day, they were truly stuffed. And it felt like they were old pals.

"Time to announce our winners," Aunt Mal yelled. "But first, I want to thank you all for coming. We were able to bring in $3,000 for our local beaches. That money will help protect the waters we all love. Thank you! Thank you!"

The winning dish was fried chicken.

Sara was not too surprised.

Growing up in North Carolina, she knew many people had a soft spot for the classics.

"This was pretty great," Priya said. She was helping Sara pack up the last of the pots and pans.

"Yeah, it truly was," Sara said.

"Here is my phone number," Priya told her. She handed her a slip of paper. "Maybe we can plan another?"

"Definitely!" Sara said.

She saw Aunt Mal behind them.

"Looks like Destiny's tip worked, huh?" Aunt Mal said when Priya walked away.

Sara smiled. "Yep, it really did."

From Sara's Kitchen

Servings: 35
Prep time: 5
Cook time: 30

Fried Chicken

1 chicken, cut up
3 Eggs
2 cup Flour
1 Tbsp Salt
2 tsp Pepper
1 tsp Garlic Powder
1 tsp Paprika

Instructions:

You want 2 bowls. In bowl 1, mix the eggs. In bowl 2, add the rest but not the oil. Then dip the chicken bits in the egg bowl, and then bowl 2. Fill a big pot with oil to the middle. Add the chicken to the pot for 10-15 minutes. It should be dark and crisp.

Notes:

Hi Destiny,

The cook-off went perfectly! Thank you for your tips. Here is the recipe that won the day.

Your friend, Sara

About the Authors

Jennie Ford is a mother, writer, potter, and artist. Jennie was raised in Eastern North Carolina, where the rich farming landscapes provide the backdrop to many of her stories.

As a contributor to Storyshares for many years, she will continue to compose short stories for their expanding library. Now residing in Western North Carolina, Jennie is currently writing a novel for young adult readers, which she hopes to publish in the future.

According to Jennie, "The goals of the Storyshares organization are wonderful and much needed." Jennie continues to feel pride lending her talents to the benefit of struggling and beginning readers with age appropriate and thoughtful stories. She is excited to learn that her stories may instill the love of reading in many.

James Quinton is a writer from a small town in central Massachusetts. When he's not at his desk, he's either in his garden coaxing his plants to grow or in his workshop turning salvaged wood and flea market finds into one-of-a-kind furniture and home decor.

About The Publisher

Storyshares is a nonprofit focused on supporting the millions of teens and adults who struggle with reading by creating a new shelf in the library specifically for them. The ever-growing collection features content that is compelling and culturally relevant for teens and adults, yet still readable at a range of lower reading levels.

Storyshares generates content by engaging deeply with writers, bringing together a community to create this new kind of book. With more intriguing and approachable stories to choose from, the teens and adults who have fallen behind are improving their skills and beginning to discover the joy of reading. For more information, visit storyshares.org.

Easy to Read. Hard to Put Down.